This Book Designed
just for
_____
with love from
_____

2

My
Clubhouse

REFRIGERATOR

THIS
END
UP

3

My Best Friend

that no one can see but me!

Written by
Emily T. Peterson

Illustrated by
Daryl B. Enos

Pensacola, Florida   Printed in USA
Patent Pending
ISBN 1-880453-02-09

I once had a best friend
that no one could see except me.
His name was Burnie.

YOU ARE
MY BEST
FRIEND

We did everything together.

Sometimes, especially on windy days, we would ride our bikes to the park to fly kites.

Sometimes we would watch cartoons on TV
and eat lots and lots of popcorn.

Sometimes we would just read our

favorite books and play games in my room.

10

Burnie was truly the best friend I ever had.

But sometimes
Burnie would
get both of us
into trouble.

BURNIE

It was never my fault.

I tried to tell everyone that Burnie didn't
mean to leave the golf clubs
in the backyard.

"A dragon has to learn
that you are supposed to put things back...

where you found them,"
I explained.

I tried to explain how Burnie didn't mean to poke a hole in <u>Grandmother's</u> favorite hat.

"A dragon loves to play dress up and look at himself in the mirror," I thought. "Burnie just forgot about the horn on his head."

I tried to tell my neighbor that Burnie didn't mean to trample her flower bed.

"A dragon has such terribly big feet," I apologized.

Burnie didn't mean to break the pretty lamp.

"A dragon is just too big to play indoors," I said, shaking my head sadly.

We were both sent to our room anyway.

Burnie and I were sad.
We were so sad
we didn't even
want to read
our books,
play games
or watch TV.

After we were tucked into bed that night, Burnie and I were given a heart to heart talk.

"Dragons like to play in open fields and tall mountains," we were told. "I think it's time for Burnie to go home. I'll bet he misses his dragon friends."

Burnie and I just listened.

Later,
Burnie and I
had a long talk.

"I do miss my dragon friends," Burnie said.
"You are growing up and soon you won't
need me anymore. It is time for me to go."

I helped Burnie pack his suitcase.

Then he opened the window and flew away.

Don't forget
to write!

I waved and waved
until I couldn't see him anymore.

I have many new friends now,
and we have lots of fun together.

But sometimes I think about Burnie and wonder what kind of games dragons play in the open fields and tall mountains.